SILVER RIBBON SKINNY

The towpath adventures of Skinny Nye, a muleskinner on the Ohio & Erie Canal, 1884.

Marilyn Weymouth Seguin

BRANDEN PUBLISHING COMPANY
Boston

© Copyright 1996
by Marilyn Weymouth Seguin

Library of Congress Cataloging-in-Communication Data:

Seguin, Marilyn.
  Silver ribbon Skinny : the towpath adventures of Skinny Nye, a muleskinner on the Ohio & Erie Canal, 1884 / Marilyn Weymouth Seguin.
     p.   cm.
  Includes bibliographical references (p.).
  ISBN 0-8283-2020-9 (alk. paper)
  1. Nye, Pearl R., 1872-1950--Fiction.
  2. Ohio and Erie Canal (Ohio)--History--Fiction.
  I. Title.
PS3569.E454S5   1996
813'.54--dc20   96-13654
                                                     CIP

BRANDEN PUBLISHING COMPANY
17 Station Street
Box 843 Brookline Village
Boston, MA 02147

Dedication

In memory of the "canawlers," the people who worked on the Ohio & Erie Canal and to those who dwelled along its towpath.

Contents

Prologue 5
Map 7
A Brief Chronology 8
Song *The Old Canal* by Captain "Skinny" Nye 10
Chapter 1 14
Chapter 2 18
Chapter 3 23
Chapter 4 30
Chapter 5 34
Chapter 6 40
Chapter 7 44
Chapter 8 50
Chapter 9 53
Chapter 10 58
Chapter 11 64
Epilogue 68
Photos 70
Glossary of Terms and Expressions 79
Selected Bibliography 85

PROLOGUE

Silver Ribbon Skinny is a work of historical fiction. The main character, Skinny Nye, is based upon the character Pearl Nye, who was born in 1872 and died in 1950, just short of his 79th birthday.

In 1939, Pearl Nye began writing a story about one of his family's trips on the Ohio & Erie Canal. More than 200 pages of the hand-written manuscript have survived and are owned by the Summit County Historical Society. Most of the people and some of the events in Silver Ribbon Skinny are based on Nye's story. Other characters (specifically, Miss Uno) and events in the book are based on accounts found in old newspaper clippings. Some are purely imaginary.

Many people helped with the research and writing of this book. Specifically, I want to acknowledge Debbie Ayers of the Cuyahoga Valley National Recreational Area for opening up the Canal Visitor Center research files; John Miller, Director of The University of Akron Archives, for making available photos and Nye's hand written diaries; The Ohio Historical Society for permission to reprint Nye's lyrics; Terry Woods, author of **The Ohio & Erie Canal, A Glossary of Terms** (Kent State University Press, 1995), who shared his research on canal language and read an early version of this book; Jack Gieck, author of **A Photo Album of Ohio's Canal Era, 1825-1913** (Kent State University Press, 1988) for

6 -- Marilyn W. Seguin

permission to reprint photos and for his wise suggestions; and Jane Turzillo who read the manuscript, made revision suggestions and contributed photos from her files. Any errors are absolutely my own.

I am grateful also to my husband, Rollie, and my children, Scott and Katy, who biked the many miles of the towpath with me as I researched this story.

Marilyn Seguin
Cuyahoga Falls, Ohio
February 14, 1996

A BRIEF CHRONOLOGY

1832
Opening of the 308-mile Ohio & Erie Canal route.

1846
The Miamis, last of Ohio's Indians, leave the state, transported by canal boat.

1847
Teenager James Garfield (20th President of the U.S.) works on the canal as a muleskinner.

1861-1865
The Civil War

1872
Pearl "Skinny" Nye's birth, on the canal boat Reform, in Chillicothe, Ohio, February 5.

1883
Nye family converts their grain boat, Tom Warren, in order to transport lumber, stone and coal on the northern division of the Ohio & Erie.

1884
The setting for the canal boat trip told in *Silver Ribbon Skinny*.

1887
Pa Nye's death. The family continues to run the boat.

1907
Canal shipments on the Ohio & Erie cease.

1913
Ohio & Erie Canal structures destroyed by flood.

1920's
Captain Pearl "Skinny" Nye lives in a converted canal boat.

1938
Captain Nye is invited to sing his canal songs at the National Folk Festival in Washington D. C.

1939
Captain Nye builds Camp Charming, his home on the old canal lock at Roscoe, Ohio.

1950
Captain Nye dies, January 4.

The Old Canal

by Captain Pearl "Skinny" Nye

1

There's a little silver ribbon runs across
                                the Buckeye State,
   'Tis the dearest place of all this earth to me,
For upon its placid surface, I was born some years ago
   And its beauty, grandeur always do I see.
Cleveland is the northern end--and Portsmouth
                                is the south,
   While its "side cuts" they are many, many, Pal.
And where'er we went we took along our home sweet
                                home, you know
   In those balmy days upon the old canal.

Chorus

There's naught in all creation that to this can compare.
   Good times, rounds of pleasure, were our lot,
                                    dear pal.
No other people e'er were known to have such times as we
   In those balmy days upon the old canal.

2

There everybody had good times, a picnic all the while--
    And the scenery was entrancing all the day;
For 'twas ever new, inspiring, unexcelled,
                                  you ne'er forgot--
    There was no monotony along the way.
The rivers they would smile and flirt--such antics;
                                  oh, they cut!
    While the tumbles, dams, locks,
                      they would laugh and roar.
Everybody was "Eureka," not a care dare show his face--
    In those dear old balmy days of yore.

3

At night, when running, we would gather
                            on deck for fun--
    Stories, songs and music always in demand.
For we were night hawks, more or less;
                        'twas in the game you know,
    We were lords of all we saw or could command.
'Twas "Hello Cap!" on every side and smiles
                              all down the line,
    For the canalers brought their wealth and fame,
                                    dear pal!
And there are all the old timers I know
                                would fair return
    To those balmy days upon the old canal.

45

On the towpath I had fun, grasshopper playing tag.
    Honey, bumblebees, and yellow jackets, too.
And when a hornet's nest I'd see, oh how the stones
                                    would fly.
    Then the mules would kick and dance--

the sky was blue.
The turtles, frogs and snakes would dive
and come up with a smile.
They'd wink at me, the snakes stick out
their tongues.
The skating bugs and spiders, oh what capers
they would cut
'Twas amusing just to watch their skip and run.

49

The thoughts of those old days sure fill
and thrill me like a flood!
I was just a child of nature, simple, kind.
For everything along the way just seemed to smile
and speak,
Nite and day, the serenade was great--sublime!
I learned how all the creatures lived, their habits,
voices and song.
They knew I was their friend--and oft they would eat
from my hand,
In those dear old days upon the old canal.

50

The locks were oft our swimming holes, we'd empty,
fill at will
In the upper, lower jaws, all kinds of fun.
Turning the flip-flops, diving from the foot-bridge,
balance beams,
Snubbing the posts and gates, the couping stones
would run.
We'd spring the paddles, make it rough, 'twas something
like a storm.
None ventured but good swimmers, dear old pal.
Oh days of heaven, here on earth, I never will forget.

Take the world, but give me the old canal.

51

We were a happy family, there were many boys and girls
    But dear father, mother had a watchful eye,
We ran and played all o'er the boat, but accidents
        would come,
    Then our clothes would be put out on the line
        to dry.
We had our courses, work and play, so everyone
        had fun,
    'Twas quite systematic, loving service, pal
And all the comforts of those days--we had aboard
        our boat;
    You may have the world--give me the old canal.

74

Oh yes, the Ohio and Erie Canal can well be proud,
    For her past is glorious! Matchless! Oh so grand!
I know her well from A to Z--describe her every mile
    And I was zealous--always for her I would stand!
In childhood, youth, maturity, I always loved her dear,
    But now my heart is often saddened, pal.
Oh, how I wish that all might know and love her as I do
    And would take a trip upon the old canal.

Excerpted from "Captain Pearl R. Nye's Ohio Canal Songs," *The Gamut*, Fall 1983. (Used with permission).

*"There's a little silver ribbon runs across the Buckeye State,
'Tis the dearest place of all this earth to me"*

From *The Old Canal*, by Captain Pearl "Skinny" Nye.

Chapter 1

I guess life on a canal boat was just about the best life a boy or girl could ever want. I was born on my parents' canal boat on February 5, 1872, the fifteenth child of Mary and William Nye. All of us Nye kids grew up on the canal, all 'cept Wilma, our little sister who got sick and died.

By the time I was born, there were so many Nye children that Pa had to operate two boats and with the help of my oldest brother, Billie, ran 'em both for awhile. We lived on those boats year round, and we were never bored, cause there's always something to do on the canal. By 1884, when I was twelve, Billie was running one of our boats by himself, and Ma and Pa and seven of us younger Nye kids lived on the other boat, the Tom Warren. Our dog Guess lived with us and so did our mules.

The Tom Warren was a three-cabin freighter. The rear cabin was the kitchen during the day, and Ma and Pa and my sisters Cora and Jessie slept there at night. The hatch to the cabin was on the roof and we had to climb down a ladder to get in the cabin when the Warren was loaded. In 1884, we was haulin' lumber in the holds between the cabins. Us boys slept in the front cabin with Guess. The mules' stable was the center cabin, and there was a catwalk over the tops of the cabins, so's we could always get around the boat pretty good. We had everything we needed on the Warren, and what we didn't have, we didn't need. The canal life kept us busy and happy.

In summers, we could swim and catch turtles or just lay on the deck and daydream as our canal boat drifted down that old silver ribbon, which was what we called the Ohio & Erie Canal. We fished off the bow as Pa steered us through the slow, current-less water. With all of us kids fishing at once, we could pull up a big mess of fish in no time. We caught rock bass and blue gills, mostly, and Ma and my oldest sister Cora fried 'em up in cornmeal for our dinner. Oh my, they were delicious. Sometimes we traded the fish for other meat and vegetables with farmers who lived along the towpath. We never went hungry on the canal.

In winters when the canal iced in until the spring thaw, we still fished in the canal, cutting a hole in the black ice so's we could sink our lines. Pa liked to winter over in Akron, so's the younger children could go to the Perkins school and my older brothers and Pa could find work in the rubber shops. But all us Nyes, even Ma and Pa, liked to skate on the frozen canal in the evenings, afterwards warming ourselves by the bonfire Pa built on the towpath.

We ran our canal boat from March through December. Unless we were in a big hurry to deliver a load, we traveled only in the daylight and tied up in the evening. All along the Ohio & Erie Canal, there were boys and girls living in the towns and on farms, and we sometimes got together to swim or fish. We called those kids "town jakes" and mostly they looked down on us canalers, but

I guess they thought we were OK when they wanted to get a ball team together.

Sometimes, canalers from other boats came over to visit us, for we Nyes were all very musical, and we were famous up and down the Ohio & Erie for our singing and dancing gatherings. My baby sister Jessie loved to dance, so just about every night in the summers, she'd fetch Pa his fiddle and beg him to play so's she could dance. Pa usually made a big show about not wantin' to play, but then he would play his fiddle and Ma and me sang old songs or made up new ones, and we all danced. Sometimes, we'd dance so hard that we loosened the deck boards and if it rained that night, Ma and Pa and my sisters would get wet as they slept, for their beds was just below the deck where we danced.

From the time I was eight years old, my favorite canal job was driving our mules that pulled the boat over that old silver ribbon. That's how I got my name "Skinny" cause the town jakes call mule drivers "mule skinners" even though no canaler would ever use that term. For me, though, the nickname stuck, and even Ma and Pa called me Skinny. I thought Skinny was a whole lot better name for a boy than Pearl, which was my real name.

Our best mules were named Lookout and Son-of-a-Gun. Lookout was a quiet, hard worker, but Son-of-a-Gun was another story. He was stubborn and balky, and if I followed that old broomtail too close along the towpath, he would kick and reel. He was pretty skittish for an old guy, too, and whenever he'd hear gunshot or firecrackers, he'd bolt. Our other pair of mules was named Pete and Repeat, and they was both dumb as a box of rocks. My sister Cora didn't like mules, not a one of them. She said mules couldn't be trusted. Cora could find more things wrong with our mules than there is in a mule to be wrong, but I liked 'em well enough, 'specially Lookout and Son-of-a-Gun.

We spelled our mule teams every six or eight hours. When one pair of mules was towin', the other pair was restin' in the center cabin on board the Warren. On the towpath, we hitched our mules in tandem, one behind the other, so there would be plenty of room to pass if we met a mule team towing in the opposite direction. Lookout didn't like snakes, hated 'em worse than my sister Cora hated 'em and that was a lot. Whenever I was driving Lookout, I sent our old dog Guess ahead of the mules to scare the snakes off the towpath. Whatever their failures, I liked all our mules, and I did my best thinking when I was walking the towpath behind Lookout and Son-of-a-Gun.

My dream was to one day be the captain of my own canal boat and live out my life on the silver ribbon. I loved the canal life--we all did, and we wanted it to last forever. But by the time I was twelve years old, the railroads had taken so much of the canal business that Pa said we might have to give up the boating life. It was my biggest fear. That was the summer I learned how to face up to all my fears.

*"But I can not bring back the past,
Tho' it was great while it did last,
I know such thoughts are often vain,
But I love to live it o'er again."*

From *Towpath Circus*, by Captain Pearl "Skinny" Nye.

Chapter 2

"Do you ever wish nothing would change? That time would just stop?" I asked my family at dinner one night after we had loaded lumber on our canal boat. Cora was helping Ma with supper. My brothers Lowell, Warren, George and Del were wolfing down their "Lake Erie boats" (biscuits) and "red turkey" (boiled beef).

"I do. I do," said my baby sister Jessie. She always took whatever we said real literal like. "I could keep eating Cora's "Punch and Judy" (homemade noodles) till I bust!" Everyone laughed. Jessie was always saying cute things--she was the real pet of the family.

Ma said, "Change is what life is all about, Skinny. That's what makes living so exciting--you never know when you start out just where life's going to take you."

"I want to know where I'm going before I get there," I said. "Just like the Tom Warren. We always know where our canal boat's going to take us whenever we start out. We know where we've been and we know where we're a goin'. I like that."

Pa looked at me across the table and said, "Nothing ever stays the same, Skinny, especially on the canal. I been boating on the Ohio & Erie Canal all my life and I can tell you that things have changed mightily since I started work on the big ditch. Things are still changing and the canalers got to change to keep up with the times."

I knew Pa was talking about the railroad. Before the railroad butted in on the canal trade, our boats used to haul grain on the southern part of the Ohio & Erie Canal, from Chillicothe all the way to Columbus. But when the railroads were built, the trains took all the grain business cause trains were faster, so Ma and Pa had the top deck ripped off the Tom Warren and built the three cabins instead. It was old Mr. Kellogg and his men that did the job. When those men started cuttin' into the deck, Jessie got real mad and she tried to fight those doing it. The boat looked cockeyed and crazy to me, too, when it was all done, and it spoiled the beauty of our white fairy palace. But it had to be done, and the changing from hauling grain to general freight was the cause. That had happened when I was ten. Now I was twelve, and we was working the canal between Cleveland and Akron, hauling lumber south and coal or stone north.

"One of these days, I'm going to build us an electric mule, so's we can retire Lookout and Son-of-a-Gun, and we can haul grain again on the canal. My electric mule will run ten times as fast as the trains," I declared. "In fact, my mule will probably put the railroads out of business!" Everyone chuckled at my words, but I was dead serious.

"That's plain stupid, Skinny. An electric mule! You're such a dreamer," said Cora as she helped Ma clear the table of the supper dishes. Jessie and my brothers looked as though they thought it was a stupid idea, too, but they didn't say anything.

"Your brother is not a dreamer, Cora. He just has an analytical mind and a sensitive soul," said Ma. Ma always stuck up for me when my brothers or Cora teased me. Jessie never teased.

"If he's so smart, then why do you let him stay home from school in the winter, when the rest of us have to go?" said Cora. "Maybe he is smart, but seems to me he has as much to learn as the rest of us."

I glared at Cora. She could be such a pain.

"He doesn't go to school because the town children tease him and his teachers don't understand his spells," said Ma. "Skinny's spells don't mean he's not smart, Cora. Skinny knows as much as the rest of you from what I teach him at home. And he reads more books than all of you Nye children put together."

Truly, my spells were a source of great shame to me. The spells started when I was two years old, after I fell off our canal boat into the Ohio River. All my older brothers and sisters were playing "Clear the Deck." In that game, whoever jumps into the water last is a rotten egg. Of course, at two, I was too young to be playing that game, but when I saw all my brothers and sisters jumping into the water, over the side I went too.

My bother Del saw me fall, and he dragged me out of the water, but not before I'd swallowed plenty of muddy Ohio River. I was unconscious for days and everyone thought I would die, but I didn't. After I came to, though, I began to have the spells. That was why Ma and Pa called me their "hothouse plant." Some folks, they said, just need a little extra protection so's they can grow up and be strong like the others.

Sometimes the spells lasted for only a few minutes and I'd get all dizzy and see spots before my eyes, and the colors of things would get all strange. Other times, the spells lasted for several days and I'd have to go off by myself until my ears stopped ringing and my head quit pounding. Ma and Pa tried to keep everyone quiet and away from me during those times, but that wasn't so easy to do with so many of us living on the Tom Warren.

"I'm not afraid to go to school, Cora. And I know a lot more than you do," I shouted at my sister. I wanted to wring her neck, I was so mad.

"I've heard enough teasing for this day," said our Pa. "We should all turn in early tonight. Tomorrow, we begin our run to Akron and I have a surprise for all of you. This trip is not going to be like any other trip you've ever taken on the canal. This trip is special. Now go to bed, all of you, and I'll tell you all about it in the morning."

That night I had a hard time gettin' to sleep. I shared a cabin with Warren, George, Del and Lowell. Guess slept with us if there was weather, but on nice nights like tonight he'd sleep on the deck so's he could guard the Tom Warren. Lowell fell asleep right away, but Del, Warren and George were buzzin' about Pa's surprise.

"What do you think Pa is cooking up for this haul?" Del asked no one in particular. Del was sixteen that summer, and he had a lot of responsibility on our boat already.

"Maybe we're not goin' to Akron this time. Maybe we'll keep on goin' south till we reach Portsmouth," said Warren, who was a year younger than me. Ma and Pa had named my brother Warren after our boat the Tom Warren, and he was real proud of that.

"Could be Ma and Pa are wantin' to take a vacation from hauling cargo on the canal," suggested George. "Pa's been real tired looking lately. Loading lumber and stone is a lot harder work than loading grain, even if Pa does have us boys to help him."

I lay there in my berth, thinkin' about Pa's surprise. I sure didn't want no vacation from the canal, I can tell you. The canal life was my delight. When I finally fell asleep, I dreamed that I was the captain of my own canal boat, the best boat on the whole stream. In my dream, I skillfully navigated my boat through the water, never touching the banks on either side. The other canalers smiled and waved at me from their boats, shouting "Hey, Cap'n Nye!" as I maneuvered through the locks and across the aqueducts that carried the old silver ribbon over the rivers and streams of Ohio.

Sometimes dreams come true in ways you don't expect.

*"But a better life could never come.
Let others do as they choose, dear Pal.
But I will stay on the old canal."*

From *A Canal Dance*, by Captain Pearl "Skinny" Nye.

Chapter 3

Next morning when I stepped out of bed into a puddle of water, I knew right away we wouldn't be gettin' an early start.

"Del, get the medicine spoon. We've got a leak," Pa yelled from the cabin roof over my head.

The other boys were up before me. I liked to sleep late, and I was quite often the very last of the Nyes out of bed in the morning. I pulled on my pants and scrambled on deck to see what was goin' on.

"Warren, pack that medicine spoon with sawdust. Del, get ready to swim. We've got to fix this leak before we begin our run." Pa was barking out orders to my brothers. I smelled the good smells of bacon and coffee coming from the kitchen cabin. Ma and my sisters must be up, too. I decided to watch Pa and Del fix the leak before I went for my breakfast.

On deck, my brother Warren packed dry sawdust into a small, open wooden box. Us Nyes always used a sawdust-filled box for a medicine spoon, though some canalers swore that a bag filled with manure was a better cure for a leaky boat.

"I'm all set, Pa," Del said as he jumped over the side of the boat into the canal. Del loved to swim--he was the best swimmer I ever saw, and he could hold his breath for a long time. Scared Ma plenty of times when Del went underwater and didn't come up right away.

Warren leaned over the side and handed down the medicine spoon to Del.

"The leak is right next to the rear cargo hold, just like I showed you. You think you can find it OK from the underside?" Pa asked Del.

Del just grinned back at Pa, and clutching the medicine spoon, he dove under the Tom Warren. When Del passed the medicine spoon under the boat, the inflow of the leaking water would suck the sawdust out of the box and into the cracks of the boat. When that sawdust got thoroughly wet and swelled, it would plug the leak.

It wasn't long before Del surfaced and Warren and I helped him climb aboard. Pa inspected the leak and said the medicine had already worked its cure and we should all gather for breakfast so's he could tell us his surprise.

"Your Ma and I wanted to make this trip a special one for all the Nyes," Pa began and he winked at Ma. "We decided that we'll be in no special hurry this trip so that each of you children can take turns being the captain of the Tom Warren. Del, Cora, Lowell, George, Skinny, Warren and Jessie--you'll each have a turn," said Pa.

Ma and Pa couldn't have given us kids a better surprise than that, now I tell you. A canal boat captain was some powerful figure in our world. Captain was the one who took charge of everything on the boat, includin' giving all the crew their own special jobs. We whooped and shouted our joy and clapped each other on the back. Guess barked and barked, and even when we kids quieted down, Guess kept barking. We were all anxious to get underway.

"We will start our trip with Captain Jessie Violet Nye," said Pa. Jessie's eyes got big as plates. "She will choose her own crew from the rest of the family. Your Ma and I are no exceptions, so choose who you want, Jessie. Let no one influence her decision," said Pa to the rest of us, who were already yelling out what we wanted to do on crew.

Jessie was not one for thinking over long about much, and she soon made up her mind.

"I want Del for my bowman," she declared. It was up to the bowman to leap off the boat at each lock and snub the bow with a line to keep the boat from crashing into the closed lock gates in front of it.

"I want Ma as my hairpin," Jessie continued. Ma looked pleased that Jessie wanted her as the cook, even though it was Cora who was the best cook I ever knew, then or since.

"Lowell will be my mule driver, and I want Skinny for my steersman," Jessie finished, looking proudly at her crew. I was brimming with excitement to be steersman. The steering of the canal boat is at the back, or stern, where I would guide the boat to keep it from bumping the canal banks.

"I think you made some good choices, Captain," said Pa. "Now I'm going on deck and I'll leave Captain and crew to their operations."

The first "operation" was getting the loaded Tom Warren weighed so we could determine the tolls for using the canal. I steered the Tom Warren into the weigh lock, no problem, and Del snubbed the boat to a stop. Then the weigh-lock tender closed the gates in front of and behind the Tom Warren, and emptied the water out of the lock until our boat was resting on a giant scale. The weigh-lock tender had a list of what all the freighters on the Ohio & Erie weighed when they were empty, and he subtracted the Tom Warren's empty weight from what the boat weighed loaded in order to determine the pay rate. Pa signed the weight statement that said what toll we would pay once we got to Akron, and the lock refilled until we were floating once again.

Soon we were underway, floating through the city of Cleveland. As steersman, most of my work was making sure the boat didn't run into the side of the canal. You see, the mules pulled from the towpath on only one side of the canal, and if you didn't steer the boat, it would run right into the towpath side bank, following after those mules. Steering was a bit tricky once you reached a lock, which was a set of wooden gates that controlled the water level. The canal got real narrow when you were locking through, as we called it, and the steersman had to be careful not to let the boat hit up against the sides of the stone locks. The locks could raise or lower a canal boat just like a set of stairs can take a person up or down, depending on his wish. I had locked through plenty by the time I was twelve, so I wasn't worried about locks. It was the aqueducts that scared me. I'd never navigated the aqueducts before.

As Jessie's steersman, I'd have to steer the boat through the Mill Street Aqueduct, and it took a pretty good steersman to get a boat over that big trough of water without bumping the sides. Four miles beyond that was the Tinker's Creek Aqueduct, and even the best steersman on the Ohio & Erie had a hard time getting through the Tinkers Creek Aqueduct without a jolt or two.

I settled in at the tiller, intent in my steering and wanting to show Pa that I could do a good job. And I was, too. Doing a good job, that is. Pa joined me on deck as we were locking through at Rathbun's Lock.

"Enjoying yourself, Skinny?" he asked, squinting into the bright sunlight.

"You bet, Pa," I said. I sure was full of myself just then. We were still in Cleveland, and for a while we watched the people riding by us on Harvard Avenue that ran alongside the canal. Pa said that before the canal, Cleveland was nothin' but a village and Akron was but a shanty town. T'was the canal that brought prosperity and growth to the city of Cleveland on Lake Erie and to other cities along the canal.

"Canal's the best thing this country's ever done," said Pa, as he relaxed on the deck beside me.

"Sure must've taken a long time to dig this old ditch," I marveled.

"Two years just to dig the section from Cleveland to Akron that we'll be on this trip," said Pa. "They say there's a dead canal builder buried for every mile of the canal. Some died from too much alcohol, sure, but most died from accidents and sickness. Cholera epidemic of 1832 took hundreds. Buried some of 'em right in the canal bed before it was watered. The rest they buried along the banks of the canal, right where they died," Pa said.

Pa's words made me feel creepy as I sat thinking about all the dead bodies we might be floatin' over. I was glad for Pa's company, but I wanted to change the subject.

"Lot of folks died buildin' the canal, but it brought lots of folks in, too, ain't that so, Pa?"

"Brought folks in, sure--also took folks out. When I was a boy, I saw the last of the Indians leave Ohio forever. They was Miamis. And you know how they traveled, Skinny? They went out in three canal boats. Saw them myself in the fall of 1846. Government just loaded the Indians on those boats and took 'em to Cincinnati. They had their blankets and bows and arrows, and they looked like wild hunters, but Ohio wasn't good hunting ground anymore. Government resettled them in Kansas, finally, I heard," said Pa.

I listened to Pa as I steered the Tom Warren, thinking about the Miamis. They had probably felt about the canal the same way as me and Pa felt about the railroad. I s'pose that whenever there's a change, there's opportunity for some and an end of things for others.

We passed Six Mile Bridge where I once caught a snail while fishing. Cora had laughed at me and teased me for catching such a slow thing with a hook, but Pa had said it took a good fisherman to do that.

We locked through just fine at Eight-mile lock. Soon, I could see the Mill Street Aqueduct in the distance where the water narrowed down to a trough hardly as wide as the Tom Warren. I sure was glad that Pa was with me, so's he could help me out if I got in trouble. By the time we were within a few yards of the mouth of the aqueduct, I was gripping the tiller so tight that I couldn't even feel my fingers. I wasn't trustin' myself to enter that aqueduct without bumping up against the sides, no way, so I asked Pa to take the helm.

"Skinny, I know you plan to captain your own canal boat some day, so you've got to know how to steer through the aqueducts. You can do this now," said Pa. I believed him.

I concentrated. I concentrated so hard, **I willed** that boat to go straight. We floated over Mill Street, with me as the steersman. Yes, I could do it. I was going to be the best captain on the canal one day, and I was about to burst with the pure joy of the thought.

It was coming out of the aqueduct when we hit the side. I was just beginning to relax when I heard Jessie yellin' up to me to steer towards the heel path, but it was too late. That old boat trembled when she bumped up against the side and I heard Del yellin' for the medicine spoon.

"'Twas 'Hello Cap!' on every side and smiles
all down the line,
For the canalers brought their wealth and fame, dear pal!
And there are all the old timers I know would fair return
To those balmy days upon the old canal."

From *The Old Canal*, by Captain Pearl "Skinny" Nye.

Chapter 4

"Good job, Mr. Steersman," Cora said sarcastically. "When I'm captain for a day, I'm certainly not going to choose Skinny for my steersman." Cora was smiling, but her words stung me.

It took nearly four hours for Pa and Del to repair the leak and everyone was cranky and anxious to get moving again. Jessie pouted. Her day as Captain wasn't turning out well and it was all my fault. I knew it and so did she. Some canal boat captain I'd grow up to be. Four aqueducts on the run from Cleveland to Akron, and I couldn't even steer through the first one. Then the shame drained away and fear took its place, because the next aqueduct was only four miles ahead and as long as Jessie was Captain, I was the steersman. Before we got underway, I hunted down Pa.

"Pa, will you be my pilot when we cross Tinker's Creek?" I asked. Sometimes canalers used professional pilots to steer boats through tricky locks. Even Pa, though he was as good a steersman as I ever knew, sometimes hired a pilot to steer the Tom Warren through the Akron locks. Those locks could be mighty tricky during busy times.

"No, Skinny, I won't. Jessie chose you as her steersman, and I will not override her decision. You will steer the boat across Tinkers Creek Aqueduct and over the Peninsula Aqueduct, if Captain Jessie decides to keep going that far," Pa said. I tried to reason with him, but he left so's he wouldn't have to listen to me nag him anymore.

Pa thought I could do it. If I concentrated, I could do it. I began to believe it. I'd show that big-mouth Cora that I could do it. I began to relax as we made our way along the canal, busy with life on this fine summer afternoon.

We met plenty of boats coming, hauled by sweating teams. As the boat heading upstream, the Warren had the right of way. Whenever we met another boat then, it was s'posed to pull over to the heelpath and drop its towlines so's I could steer the Warren right over its ropes.

We locked through Twelve-Mile Lock at Valley View. Locks was numbered, all of them, but some locks had special names on account of things that happened there at one time or another or because of how they looked. There was Pancake Lock, for instance, named that cause the land on both sides of the canal was so flat. And there was Lonesome Lock, which everyone knew was haunted, named cause it made you feel so bad and so scared when you went through. Most everyone on the canal used names instead of numbers for the locks.

Pretty soon, I could see the aqueduct straight ahead. I could feel my hands sweatin' as I gripped the tiller and I began to get a funny feeling in my stomach. I probably would have kept on going if Del hadn't come on deck to join me just as we came close to that aqueduct. But maybe I would have done the awful thing anyway, and even today it makes me feel ashamed. But I was feeling mighty desperate as we came up on that aqueduct.

So I did something I'd never done before, and I ain't done since. I faked one of my spells. It might have worked, too, except that Cora was on to it almost from the beginning. Whenever I had my spells, I went below to my bunk so's to be out of the light mostly, cause the light made my head hurt worse. And so that day when I faked my spell, Cora stood on the deck above my bunk and said to the others, real loud to make sure I could hear:

"Skinny is just chicken, Lowell. He's not any more sick that you an' me. He's just pretending to have a spell so's he can get out of work just like he gets out of goin' to school," Cora said.

Lowell said something I couldn't make out, and then I heard George and Warren laugh real loud. They were all up there laughing at me, even Jessie. I'd show them. I decided to punish my family by not speaking to them. Then they'd be sorry. That night I put up a wall of silence between me and my family. I didn't even look at Ma when she brought me a plate of supper, nor did I answer Lowell and George and Del when they came down later to see if I was feeling better. Hurting them this way made me feel good. But then they stopped talking to me and the hurt turned against me, and I guessed hurting people you love wasn't so much fun after all.

I lay awake late into the night, thinking about what I had done. In the distance I heard thunder roll, and pretty soon the wind came whistling through the lumber stacked in the holds. Guess came to join us just as the first flash of lightening lit the cabin and without even looking at me, he jumped up to share Warren's berth. Even old Guess was disgusted at what I'd done. The storm came quickly and the sound of the rain falling on the deck of the Tom Warren made me sleepy, but I could not let go of my wakefulness, so ashamed as I was about what I'd done. I listened to the rain all night as I lay awake in my bunk, thinkin' about what a failure I was.

*"You can talk of your picnics and trips to the lake,
But a trip on the Erie you bet takes the cake."*
From **A Trip on the Erie**, collected from the singing of Captain Pearl "Skinny" Nye.

Chapter 5

I woke to the smell of smoke from the kitchen wood stove and the sound of crockery as Ma prepared our breakfast. The rain had stopped sometime after I'd finally fallen asleep, and the sun was shining. I was some hungry, so I joined my family for breakfast and declared that I was better. Cora looked at me, smirking. I smiled back at her in a real nice way. I had decided to be nice to Cora today, even after what she had said about me yesterday.

"Jessie, please don't feed Guess under the table. He won't learn any manners if you do that," said Ma as she set a plate of biscuits on the table. Guess, who was old enough to have learned all the manners he ever would learn, heard his name and woofed, thumping his tail on the floor.

"That's Captain Jessie, if you please," she shot back.

"Captain Jessie did a fine job of navigating yesterday," said Pa. "But today we will have a new crew, under the direction of --" and he paused, looking at each of us kids in turn until we squirmed in anticipation. "Captain Cora Mary Nye," Pa finished.

Cora announced her crew in a real smug way. "I want Del as my steersman and Warren as my bowman," she began. "And for my hairpin, I want--" Cora looked right at me, but I didn't flinch. I don't much like to cook, but I can if I have to. Leave it to Cora to make me hairpin just to be mean. When the others saw Cora look at me, they began to protest.

"No, no, don't pick Skinny for hairpin," squealed Jessie. "Skinny always leaves lumps in the forget-me-knots (mashed potatoes). Yuck!"

"And his pleasant dreams (beans) give us nightmares," said George. Everyone was laughing. To the town folks, our canal talk was backwards, but I thought it was rich, and I was laughing as hard as the rest, even if it was me who was the butt of their jokes.

"Oh, all right," said Cora. "Skinny can do what he likes best--he'll be my driver. And my hairpins will be Pa and Jessie." And everyone groaned, knowing Pa and baby Jessie weren't much better at cookin' than I was.

Soon after breakfast was cleared, we began to make ready for gettin' underway. I was mighty glad Cora wanted me to drive cause it was a fine day. The heavy rain from the night before had washed the air clean and fresh. I just loved walkin' the towpath on a summer's day, listenin' to the birds sing, watchin' for deer that sometimes sneaked to the canal to drink early in the morning. On a day like this, it was enough for me just to walk along the towpath in the sun and simply be.

Soon, we approached the lock at Alexander's Mill. The driver and mules always got a little break when a canal boat was locking through, cause they had to stop while the bowman navigated the boat through the lock. I unhitched the mules, Del steered the boat into the lock chamber and Lowell swung down the watering buckets, so's I could give Lookout and Son of a Gun a drink. Warren, the bowman, jumped off the boat and snubbed the Tom Warren to a complete stop by wrapping the heavy line around two round, wooden posts sunk into the ground and marked with the grooves of countless ropes. Then Warren closed the lock gates behind the boat, opened the gate paddles in front of the boat, and the water rushed into the lock raising the boat higher and higher until the level of water in the lock was the same as the level of water in the canal ahead of us. When Warren opened the gates in front of us, I re-attached the mules, and we were through the lock and on our way once again.

We were heading towards the Pinery, and I knew that we'd probably make it to Peninsula before we stopped for the night. At Peninsula, which was a fair-sized town, there was lots to do and see. Ma and Pa could shop for supplies we'd need on the boat and us kids could eat ice cream.

I walked along the towpath behind Lookout and Son of a Gun, daydreaming about how good that ice cream was gonna taste at the end of the day. Guess romped in the field beside the canal, flushing out rabbits and pheasants, all excited to be running free. Our mules did a pretty good job on their own of pulling the canal boat steady, so long as the towpath was straight. When we came to a curve, though, I always kept a tight hold on the reins cause those mules wanted to keep on walking straight. They'd walk right into the canal if the driver didn't grab ahold of the reins and guide 'em to stayin' on the towpath. But when the towpath was straight, the driver could tie the reins to the towline and trust the mules to keep pullin' without much guidance. At the next straight stretch, I tied the reins to the towline and whistled for Guess. He came bounding out of the field, his fur covered with burrs.

"Hey, old guy," I greeted him as he bounced around me on the towpath. "You stay on the path and watch for snakes now, Guess. I'm going to look for turtles in the river."

Guess trotted along the towpath in front of the mules. I knew my team would be OK so long as Guess was scaring off snakes. Lookout was very skittish about snakes, and Son of a Gun could be.

The towpath followed the Cuyahoga River pretty close. In fact, most of the time, if you was on the towpath headin' south, you could see the river on your right and the canal on your left. Then when we crossed over the aqueduct in Peninsula, the river would be on the left and the canal on the right. There wasn't much of the towpath that didn't give a driver a good view of the river, and sometimes the river was so close that the towpath was the only ground separating it from the canal.

Whenever I was driving and we came close to the river, I liked to catch turtles. There were lots of turtles in the canal too, but they were easier to sneak up on in the river when they sunned themselves on logs that littered the banks. Snappers were the easiest to catch and they made the best eating. Some of those turtles were twenty or thirty pounds apiece, and Pa said their great size meant they were also very old, more'n a hundred years, probably. Once it was caught, it took a few days before you could eat one of those old snappers, cause it had to be put into fresh water for a few days to flush out. If you didn't flush out a snapper, it would taste real bad.

I soon spotted a big snapper sunning itself on a piece of driftwood sticking out of the muddy river bank. Slowly, I moved up on it from behind, and reached out for the tail. The tail was wet and it would be slippery. I put my hand in the water and snuck up behind the great turtle, and when I got within arm's length, I grabbed that old snapper by the base of his tail, just where it met the shell. The turtle jumped in fright, and then it arched its neck towards my hand and opened its mouth and hissed, but I held on. An angry snapper is a menace, and I'd once known one to bite a man's forefinger clean off at the second joint.

I carried the turtle by its tail back to the towpath where Guess met me. The old dog barked and barked when he saw the big snapper. Behind us, the Tom Warren moved slowly through the water, and I could see Ma and my brothers George and Lowell fishing off the stern where the fish like to follow the boat. I waved at them and held up the snapper so's they could tell Del to steer over to the towpath to get it. Yes, oh yes, we'd be eatin' plenty of water meat for supper this week. Tonight the fried crappie would taste mighty good after a long, hot day on the towpath. Topped off with ice cream, of course.

Suddenly, old Guess started barking and barking. He scooted off ahead of me on the towpath, and disappeared around the bend, but I could still hear him barking. Something was up. I looked back at the Tom Warren where know-it-all Captain Cora was with Del at the tiller, both staring straight ahead at the canal. But I was ahead of them on the towpath, and as I rounded the bend, I saw other canalers gathered on the towpath ahead. Boats were lined up along the banks of the canal, mostly loaded freighters like the Tom Warren, but there was also an excursion boat carrying sightseers and picnickers. A few of the passengers waved and shouted greetings to me as I passed them on the towpath.

Some of the drivers had already detached their mule teams and tied them to trees along the towpath. Other teams were still hitched to their boats, but the mules were just standing there on the towpath with the boats all backed up in the canal. Just then, Guess came bounding back, and I left him to watch over the mules as I ran on up the towpath to see what was up.

I ran smack into Joe Sedge, Captain of the Spirit, as he was unhitching his mule team. He recognized me right away, cause everyone on the canal just about knows everyone else.

"Young Nye! They'll have to wait a while for that lumber up in Akron. Buttermilk Falls washed sand into the canal after last night's rain storm and loaded boats can't get through. We got anyone who can drive an Irish buggy (wheelbarrow) or use an Irish piccolo and banjo (pick and shovel) workin' in shifts to dig out that bar. You'd best tell your Pa, Captain Nye, that he'll be delayed a few hours."

"Captain Cora's on this run, sir," I said to him. "I'll run back and tell her." And I did.

*"We're happy there free as the birds,
My Little Silver Ribbon."*

From *My Little Silver Ribbon*, by Captain Pearl "Skinny" Nye.

Chapter 6

Sometimes after a rainstorm like the one we'd had the night before, Buttermilk Falls overflowed into the canal, filling the canal bed with sand. Although an empty boat might float right over a sand bar, a fully loaded freighter like the Tom Warren would never make it. The Tom Warren was fourteen feet wide and eighty feet long and she rode low in the water when loaded with fifty to eighty tons of cargo. There was nothing to do but to tie up and wait while the men dug out the canal by hand, wheeling away the sand until the boats could pass through safely once again.

Cora was in a tizzy when I told her. She was giving bossy orders right and left. "Skinny, you tie up the mules. George and Warren will go on up the towpath and help the men dig. Pa and Jessie will fix lunch," said Cora. She looked real disappointed that her run as captain wasn't turnin' out right, but I was secretly pleased, cause I had plans for the afternoon. As it turned out, so did everyone else.

Ma said, "We passed an apple orchard a mile back. Lowell and I thought we'd see if the farmer there wants to trade us apples for some of our fish. With your permission of course, Captain Cora. Then your Pa and

Jessie can make us apple pie for our dinner tonight." Ma winked at us.

Jessie looked uncertain about the prospect of making pie, but Pa put his arm around her and squeezed her shoulders.

"Cobbler, we'll make. I remember my own Ma's recipe for making the best apple cobbler you'll ever taste," said Pa. "And it's real easy to make too," he added. At that, Jessie lost her worried look and she smiled at us.

I did as Cora said, and took care of Lookout and Son of a Gun. Then I went back aboard the Tom Warren. Pa and Jessie had made some sandwiches and we ate them together as we sat on the walkway above the lumber piled high on our boat. The sun was high, not much of a breeze to cool you off when the boat was sittin' still. Mosquitoes buzzed around us in the hot, humid air. I was glad Cora hadn't ordered me to help dig out the canal. It was a great day for catching more turtles, I thought, for they would be sunning themselves on the banks of the river all during the hot afternoon.

"Me and Guess are going for turtles," I announced, and whistled for the dog.

"No way," said Cora. "I'm captain today, and I say you're going for raspberries," she said. "I'll go with you. Then we can get enough for jam."

"It's too hot to berry," I protested, longing for the cool water of the river. "Besides, there are too many snakes on this level of the canal." One thing Cora couldn't stand was snakes. She just went wild when she saw one in the water or on the land, and Ma and Pa made us Nye kids promise never to bring a snake aboard the Tom Warren because of Cora's fear. And we never did, that I can recall.

"We'll take Guess to scare off the snakes," said Cora. Guess perked up when he heard his name and he wagged his tail, anxious to be off the boat and on an adventure.

"You and George can go get berries. I'll go get another turtle and then we'll have enough meat for soup," I said, real reasonable like so that Cora would see the sense in my afternoon plans. But Cora was awfully stubborn once she made up her mind.

"I'm the captain, Skinny, and you'll follow my orders today or I'll tell Pa. If you can't follow the rules of this trip, Pa will never let you have a turn as captain," said Cora. I knew she was right about that, so I resigned myself to a hot afternoon of picking raspberries with Cora.

Me and Cora and Guess walked a ways north on the towpath, the same direction we had come from that morning. After a lifetime on the old silver ribbon, we knew just where to find the best berries. Now pickin' raspberries isn't easy or fun, cause raspberries grow on thorny bushes that scratch your skin even through your clothes. Come nightfall and those little scratches sting like the devil.

Raspberries wasn't my favorite to eat, either. If you look real close at a raspberry, you can see little hairs growing out of it and although a juicy, ripe red raspberry tastes pretty good baked up in a pie or cobbler, a fresh berry has little seeds all through it that crunch when you chew 'em. I prefer strawberries over raspberries anytime, but strawberries were all gone this late in the summer.

We picked berries in silence, while Guess romped nearby. Cora didn't let him get too far away, though, cause she needed him to scare off the snakes. He bounded and barked, eager to make the acquaintance of a couple of mallards that swam away from him when he approached the bank of the canal.

The grass grew long on the river side of the towpath where we was pickin' berries. Wild flowers nodded in the sun: black eyed Susans, Queen Anne's lace and clover. The sun beat down on us and we were hot and thirsty. Guess drank his fill of the canal, but Cora and me drank from a container of fresh water we took from the barrel of water we carried with us on the Tom Warren. Ma said we could get real sick if we drank from the canal, so we never did, though we sure swallowed plenty of canal water when we were swimming in it. Guess never got sick drinkin' from the canal. Neither did Lookout or Son of a Gun. Neither did we.

We'd just about filled our berry buckets and were ready to head back to the Tom Warren when we heard Guess yelp, so we went back to the towpath to find him. Probably got stung by a bee again. But when we reached him, Guess was just standing there in the middle of the towpath, looking out across the water at the fanciest canal boat I had ever seen. At first, I thought I was gettin' a sun stroke, cause what I was seein' just couldn't be real. Me and Cora and Guess just stood there gawking as the mirage approached, floating real lazy-like along the water.

"I'm ragged, I'm ragged, I'm ragged, I know,
But it's nobody's business how ragged I go.
I eat when I'm hungry and drink when I'm dry,
If nobody kills me, I'll live till I die."

From *The Old Skipper*, by Captain Pearl "Skinny" Nye.

Chapter 7

The boat was painted red and it was so shiny that the light shimmered off the bow, making it look silver wherever the sun reflected off the water. Usually red paint turned dull real fast in the outdoors, so I guessed this boat had just been painted.

The red boat was a real blunt-bowed thing, makin' me think it had been built by Mr. Kellogg, the fellow that converted the Tom Warren. Mr. Kellogg's boats were something of a joke up and down the canal, where it was said that he just built one long boat. Then when a buyer told him how long he wanted a boat, Mr. Kellogg just sawed it off to order. The shape of Mr. Kellogg's boats made them slow and hard to tow, just like the red boat me and Cora was watchin' come at us. How it dazzled in the sunlight. Around the top of the front cabin hung a fringe with golden tassels swaying from each corner of the roof, and I thought that it looked mighty nice. I decided right then that when I was the captain of my own boat, I would paint my boat red and put fringe around the top of my cabins. That boat sure was a vision, I can tell you.

I remembered Ma telling about a mule driver who stayed out in the sun so long that he began to see things that just weren't there, and for a moment I thought that might account for what I was seein'. Glancing over at Cora, I could tell by the stupid expression on her face that she was as surprised as I was at what we were lookin' at, so I guessed I wasn't sun-touched after all.

On the towpath ahead of the boat, came a boy about my size, driving the mule team. The boy's hat and the mules' harnesses were decorated with golden tassels just like the ones on the boat. Yellow hair spilled out of his tasseled hat, and when he got close I could see he had a harmonica in his pocket. What did the town jakes make of that outfit, I wondered.

I nudged Cora. She looked real dumb standing there with her mouth open. Guess, who usually barked at just about anything that moved, was standing quietly beside us, watching the boat and the boy and the mules as they made their splendid way toward us. The boy raised his arm and said, "Hey!" when he got near us. That made Guess snap out of his surprise, and he began to bark again, bringing Cora out of her own trance.

"Quiet, Guess. Look Skinny--it's a showboat. Isn't it beautiful! Do you think Ma and Pa will take us to see a show?" Cora asked. Once Ma and Pa had taken us younger kids to a showboat to see a puppet show. Later, the adults had enjoyed a night of singing and dancing aboard the same boat. Show boats of all kinds were quite common along the Ohio & Erie Canal, especially near the bigger towns on the towpath, where the entertainment would attract the town jakes as well as the canalers.

Shows cost money, though, and I knew Pa and Ma didn't have much of it to spare, what with canal business being so bad and all us kids to feed and clothe.

The boy driver came to where we stood, and me and Cora fell into step beside him. Guess followed, sniffing at the boy's heels.

"Buttermilk Falls washed sand into the canal just ahead. Canal boats been stopped all day while the men dig her out," I said to the boy, thinking I should explain that part before introducin' us. "I'm Skinny Nye and this is my sister Cora. We're runnin' lumber from Cleveland to Akron on the Tom Warren."

"Nice to meet ya," said the boy. "I'm Curly and I'm driving for my mother, Miss Uno," he said as he nodded back in the direction of the boat. I thought it was peculiar for a boy to be callin' his own Ma "Miss" something, but I didn't say it.

"Is your mother an entertainer? What does she do, sing? Is there an acting troupe aboard, or dancers?" Cora asked, not giving Curly much of a chance to answer. Cora could get real flighty when she was excited over something.

"Miss Uno doesn't sing," said Curly. That was all.

"Ought to give a show tonight in Valley View. That's where most of the freighters are waitin' for the canal to open up again. And there's an excursion boat too, The Sylph, just loaded with rich people out to see the sights. I'll bet you could get lots of people to come to a show tonight if you tie up at Valley View," Cora said.

"Can't. We're headed for Akron," said Curly. "I expect we can get through all right. Our boat is light enough to float over a sand bar." Curly's tassels was bobbin' all over and I could see that those tassels did a good job of keeping the bugs away. Worked for the mules too. Maybe we could sew tassels to Lookout's and Son of a Gun's harnesses.

"Miss Uno has been advertising in Akron for more'n a week, and folks there will be expectin' us," Curly continued. "Folks are always linin' up to see Miss Uno, the world's greatest snake charmer."

I hooted at the look on Cora's face. I started to laugh and couldn't stop, and Curly was beginnin' to get mad, him thinkin' that I was laughin' at his Ma. Really, I just thought it was some comical that Cora had got herself all worked up over the prospect of a show only to find out the main performers was snakes. It just tickled me, was all.

Cora was unnatural quiet as we walked with Curly along the towpath, thinkin' about them snakes, I guess. Curly and I kept up a pretty good conversation the whole way, and we was old friends by the time we reached the lock. Me and Cora and Guess watched while Curly snubbed the show boat to a halt, but I helped him work the gates.

"You must meet Miss Uno," he insisted, taking each of us by the hand. Guess followed. I looked at Cora--no way Cora would ever get on a boat full of snakes.

"I'm afraid my sister is afraid of snakes, Curly," I said. "But I'd love to go aboard and meet your mother."

Cora shot me a mean look and said, "Nonsense. Don't believe Skinny--he just wants to have all the fun for himself. I would love to meet your mother, Curly."

Guess whined and whined when we left him on the towpath and boarded the show boat with Curly.

"No dogs allowed on board, that's the rule," said Curly. "He might scare the snakes."

Curly led us down the steps into the main cabin. I went down first, and Cora was right behind me. It took a while for my eyes to adjust to the darkness after being outside in the bright sunshine but I could smell coffee and something else that made me think of nutmeg. It was late afternoon now and I was hollow with hunger, not having had much appetite for the berries me and Cora had picked.

The cabin windows were covered with red curtains drawn against the heat of the day, giving a reddish cast to everything inside. At the far end of the cabin, Miss Uno reclined on a low platform. The candle on the table in front of her reflected off her golden blonde hair that rose in a halo about her head. She was wearing a red dress, trimmed in white. Her stockings were also red, with black stripes, and on her feet she wore shiny, black boots that buttoned up to where they disappeared under her dress. Around her neck hung strands of red beads, some twisted around her throat like a choker, others hung to her waist. Her beautiful red dress seemed to melt into the red velvet covering on the platform.

Curly kissed his mother on her forehead. "Mother these are my new friends, Skinny and Cora, from the freighter the Tom Warren," said Curly. Curly called her "mother" instead of "Ma" when he talked to her, and "Miss Uno" instead of "mother" when he talked about her. I thought that was odd.

Miss Uno held out her hand, and I wasn't sure if I was supposed to shake it or kiss it, so I kissed it, and I guess I wasn't wrong cause she smiled at me sweetly. Oh, she was lovely.

"How do, Miss Uno," I said, just the way Ma had taught me how to when I needed to be polite. I stared at her as my eyes slowly adjusted to the red-tinged darkness of the cabin. And as I stared, the beads around Miss Uno's neck began to move.

"Say hello to my friends, children," said Miss Uno as she slid her hands down the length of her "necklace" and lifted the head of the longest snake I'd ever seen.

Behind me, I heard a thunk and I knew we'd lost Cora.

*"The big black snake will startle you,
The copperhead, the same,
While Mr. Rattler, he will buzz,
You will not forget his name."*

From *Fairy Palace*, by Captain Pearl "Skinny" Nye.

Chapter 8

Cora finally came around, and she was plenty embarrassed at fainting, especially since I was around to see it happen. Miss Uno realized right away that Cora had fainted cause she was scared of the snake she called Fred, so she told Curly to put Fred into his cage.

"Fred didn't mean to frighten you, Cora," said Miss Uno kindly once Cora'd come around. "Fred is my steadfast companion, and I sometimes forget that he scares some people. Curly should have warned you children before you came aboard."

Cora blushed and began to stammer. "It's not just Fred. It's snakes in general, Miss Uno. They're so slimy and creepy looking. And they are always all over the towpath, sunning themselves on nice days. One time when I was little I stepped on one with my bare foot. And I was so scared, I couldn't move, and there I stood, pinning that little snake to the towpath with my toes, not daring to move," said Cora.

Cora sure could run on when she was upset, but Miss Uno acted real sorry for Cora, and she patted her back and said lots of comforting things to my sister. I could tell that Cora was real taken with the beautiful Miss Uno. So was I.

"Lots of people are afraid of snakes, child, but Miss Uno loves 'em. I love all kinds, big ones like Fred, and little ones like you see on the towpath. They are all my friends," said Miss Uno to my sister.

Cora was quite recovered now, and she said with her old spunk, "I don't care if I never see another snake again as long as I live. I never go off our boat without one of my brothers or Guess to scare off the snakes ahead of me. Guess and my brothers make such a ruckus, even the frogs in the canal stop croaking when they pass."

Miss Uno laughed right out loud at that, and the sound of her laughter was music. She sure was beautiful. Soon, we were all laughing, and folks on the towpath must have wondered what was going on inside the cabin of the show boat.

"I will give you a charm to keep the snakes away from you on the towpath, Cora. Then you can go off the boat without your noisy dog and brothers," said Miss Uno. Then Miss Uno bent down close to Cora and whispered in her ear. To my amazement, Cora got up and followed her out of the cabin, just leavin' me and Curly standin' there. Women secrets, I guessed.

I helped Curly board his mules for the night. Most folks took in their mules to the stables on board overnight so the animals could eat and rest. The afternoon had passed quickly, and I thought Ma and Pa would probably get worried about me and Cora and Guess if we didn't show up at the Tom Warren real soon. I went to fetch Cora, and found her still talking with Miss Uno back in the cabin.

"Did you get your snake charm?" I asked Cora after we were back on the towpath. She nodded and held out a shiny harmonica, just like the one I'd seen in Curly's pocket.

"Miss Uno says I don't need my brothers or Guess to scare off snakes any more cause I can play this mouth organ when I walk along the towpath, and the music will charm the snakes right back into their holes," said Cora.

"Surely you don't believe that nonsense, Cora." Cora was awful gullible, even if she was smartest of all us Nye kids.

"Doesn't matter," said Cora. "If you shine a light on the demon of darkness, it will disappear." I looked at her, not real sure where her talk was goin'. She seemed real happy and pleased with herself, smug even.

"Then maybe you need a torch, not a harmonica, to charm the snakes away," I suggested.

"I won't be needin' a snake charm anyway. I'm not afraid of snakes anymore. Miss Uno told me that when you run from something that frightens you, it will haunt you all the time, waking and sleeping. But if you face up to your fear just one time, and let it do its worst, then you can go on from there and you'll not be haunted by that fear ever again."

I marveled that a little thing like a harmonica could make Cora feel all right about snakes.

*"And so it was all along the line,
We had our fun though it rain or shine.
Our deckboats they would serve as halls,
In a corner, music; one would call."*

From *A Canal Dance*, by Captain Pearl "Skinny" Nye.

Chapter 9

By the time me and Cora and Guess got back to the Tom Warren, we was hollowed out with hunger. In between bites of supper, we told the others all about our adventure aboard the showboat with our new friends Miss Uno and Curly and Fred. Jessie begged Pa and Ma to take her to see the snake show. Unlike Cora, Jessie adored all creatures, even snakes.

"Tomorrow, we'll have the sand dug out and we'll be on our way," said Pa. "Maybe we'll get caught up with Miss Uno and friends when we reach Akron. After we get unloaded, we'll have plenty of time to visit the showboat, Jessie. Now please pass the pleasant dreams (baked beans)."

That night, we was eatin' water meat (fish) along with beans and coffee, topped off with the apple cobbler that Pa and Jessie made. To our surprise it was some good, swimmin' in rich cream.

"Mmm Mmm," said Ma. "I do believe this cobbler is the best I've ever eaten. And wherever did you get the cream, hairpin Jessie?"

"Got it from a farmer on the heel path side of the canal," said Jessie. "Me and Del traded him the fish we caught this afternoon."

Ma wasn't one to let things slip by. "Del and I," Ma corrected her gently.

Jessie said, "No, Ma, you wasn't there. It was me and Del who got the cream." And we all laughed at Jessie, who enjoyed the attention and came out of her pout about not gettin' to go to Miss Uno's show that night.

That evening there was a lot of visitin' up and down the towpath where all the boats was tied up waiting to get over the sand bar in the morning. There must've been twenty-five or thirty boats all tied up along our level, freighters as well as excursion boats. Folks who wanted to sing and dance came aboard the Tom Warren, for us Nyes was famous all up and down the Ohio & Erie for lovin' music.

Pa knew just about every song ever written, I guess. Someone would call out the name of a tune and Pa would play it on the harmonica or fiddle, while the rest of us sang and danced. Sometimes we made up the words as we went along, and sometimes we sang old favorites so that everyone could sing together. We had a song for every occasion, but my favorites were songs about the canal life.

"How do you ever remember all the words to so many songs?" a visitor asked me that evening at the party. Ma heard the question, and she winked at me. Me and Ma (Ma and I) had a secret system for remembering the words to songs we'd hear from other canalers or travelers. Our secret was that we took turns memorizing verses, Ma committing the first verse to memory, then me takin' the next verse and so on, until between us we committed the whole song to memory. Then as soon as we could, we'd write down what we remembered into a book. After we'd sung the verses out of the book a few times, we'd both usually committed the whole song to memory forever.

Folks living in the farms along the towpath didn't get much sleep that evening, as the singing and dancing went late into the hot, humid night. Heat lightning webbed the sky, and the canalers worried that another thunderstorm might wash more sand into the canal before morning. But it stayed dry, and the parties continued. I looked across the water of the canal and wondered if Miss Uno and Curly could hear us from their boat a few miles back on the towpath.

After the singing and dancing had tuckered folks out, they broke into smaller groups to "exchange news of the canal" as Ma said. Pa called it "gossipin'." It happened that night that Ma and some of the other women were gathered in the cabin of the Tom Warren. Cora and Jessie were spending the night with friends on another boat, and the rest of us Nye kids had been sent to bed after the singing was done, but we couldn't sleep. That's when Warren and me snuck out of our cabin so's we could "spy" on Ma and her visitors.

Warren was just a year younger than me, but he was a lot stronger. In the dark, the two of us rearranged some of the lumber in the hold so that we could hide down inside the crack between the boards and still hear and see what was goin' on in the cabin where Ma was exchangin' the news with her friends.

Canal folk have their own special language, and you got to be one of us to really understand what you hear from a canaler.

Me and Warren heard more'n we wanted to that night, and we understood all of it.

"Say, you know that old lock tender back at Valley View was always moss backed (drunk) good and plenty. I could always tell because he had a long wind (strong breath) that almost stifled me," said a woman called Grandma, the hairpin from the freighter Soul Searcher.

"His wife was the one who tended the lock most times. A good soul, though she was peculiar--a dried beef (smoker) and chimney cleaner (snuff user). At least she was no hot water bug (drunk) like her husband," said Ma. Then the voices dropped so low that Warren and I couldn't hear what they said, but it sure must've been comical, cause they all hooted and laughed for a good while.

I looked out through the cracks between the boards that hid me and Warren. The oil lamp in the cabin threw a rectangle of yellow light against the lumber.

"I heard Captain Perry of the Naragansett was fittin' Lonesome Lock one night last month and he found a dead man laying near the upper snubbing post. His eyes was open," said Grandma.

"Course his eyes was open. How else could he have seen the dead man?" someone else asked.

"Don't be dense Vera. I meant the dead man's eyes was open. If you die with your eyes open, they stay open till someone closes them," replied Grandma.

"Why was Captain Perry fitting the lock? Where was his bowman?" Ma asked.

"Bowman was too scared. Lots of crew won't work through Lonesome Lock at night," said Grandma.

I shot a look at Warren, and his eyes looked real big and shiny in the moonlight. I shivered even though the night was still warm. Everyone who worked this section of the canal knew that Lonesome Lock was haunted by the ghosts of more'n a dozen victims who were murdered there. Even the town jakes who lived nearby stayed away from Lonesome Lock after sunset.

Grandma said, "Captain Perry pulled the body out of the water and it was naked. The murderer took every stitch of clothes that poor soul was wearin'. They say the body was pure white, and all wrinkled like your hands get on wash day."

Next to me in our dark cubbyhole, Warren began to shake all over. At first I thought he was scared, but then I realized he was laughing. He began to snort from trying to hold it back.

"Stop it, Warren. They'll hear, and if they find us here, we'll be in for it," I hissed. But Warren kept on laughing, and soon he began to make little wheezing noises as he lost control completely.

"We'd better get out of here," I whispered and I lifted the top board of our hiding place. We crept back to our cabin.

"What's the matter with you anyway," I asked Warren when we were back in our bunks. He was still laughing, and about to wake up our sleeping brothers.

"I was just picturing in my mind the ghost of that poor murdered fella, all naked and white and wrinkly, and it struck me funny. Ghost is only scary to me if it has its clothes on. A naked ghost is just funny, that's all," explained Warren. And he began to laugh even harder, and he was probably still laughing after I finally fell asleep.

*"He's proud of his record, Old Son-of-a-Gun,
Has good traits abundant, a friendly old guy,
But he's an old rounder, keep open your eyes."*

From *My Old Canal Mule*, by Captain Pearl "Skinny" Nye.

Chapter 10

The next day was another beauty, hot and bright. The men had cleared the sand from Buttermilk Falls out of the canal and all the canalers were buzzing around their boats, anxious to be underway. By then, there were forty or fifty canal boats, mostly freighters, backed up on our side of the lock. No telling how many more were waitin' to lock through from the other direction.

"It'll be late afternoon before we get underway, I'm afraid," said Pa at breakfast. "Too many boats waiting."

"Pa, who will be captain of the Tom Warren today?" asked Jessie as she helped Pa clear the table. Officially, Pa and Jessie was still hairpins until the new crew was picked.

"Today our commander will be Captain Warren," said Pa. Warren smiled, but he looked real tired from bein' up so late spying on the gossipers. "If we're lucky, we can make it to Johnny Cake Lock tonight. Then we'll be able to unload in Akron tomorrow," said Pa.

"And then can we see Miss Uno charm the snakes?" Jessie asked. Jessie just wasn't goin' to let up on Pa till he took her to that snake charmin' show.

"We'll see," said Ma, "but now let's have Captain Warren of the Tom Warren choose his crew so we can make ready.

Warren wasn't one to waste time. He announced, "I want Jessie and Pa for my steersmen, and George and Lowell can alternate as bowman. Cora, I want you for hairpin, and find something tasty to do with them raspberries you and Skinny picked yesterday. Ma can take a break today since she was up so late exchangin' news."

We all laughed about that, but Warren laughed the loudest. When he shot me a look, I knew he was thinkin' about the naked ghost.

Warren collected himself. "Skinny, you can be my driver," Warren finished. And that was just fine by me, cause there wasn't one thing I liked to do any better than drivin' our mules along the towpath on a fine, sunny day like today.

Pa had been right. It was real late afternoon before we could get started. The Tom Warren was one of the last of the backed up boats to get underway, and the traffic on the canal was sparse cause the others had cleared out. The canal shimmered in the afternoon light and cicadas were singin' in the trees along the towpath.

In the town of Valley View, a road follows the canal just past Alexander's Mill. Then the towpath veers off into the forest, following the river. This section of the canal is called "The Pinery," and it's mighty peaceful.

The Pinery towpath was my favorite level on the entire silver ribbon, and I sure was grateful to God and to Warren for lettin' me be the one to be drivin' over it on this day. The towpath followed the Cuyahoga River so close that in some parts the towpath was the only land between the river and the canal. Walkin' through the Pinery made me feel like I was walkin' on the water itself.

In the shady parts, the towpath was covered with moss and I took off my shoes so's I could feel the soft, green moss cool my feet. Ma didn't like us to go barefoot on the towpath, though. For one thing, there were too many snakes. For another thing, we Nye kids often had what Ma called the "cow itch," which made the foot all tender and hurtful between the little toe and the one next to it. Ma would put cornstarch and iodine on the cow itch, and whew, did that iodine ever sting! But today I chanced getting the cow itch and took off my shoes, tying the shoestrings to the mules' wiffletree so's I wouldn't lose the only pair of shoes I owned.

Pa said that President Garfield used to drive mules over the Pinery towpath when Garfield was a boy working the canal with his uncle. One time, Pa said, Garfield got his lines tangled with the lines from another team coming down the towpath in the opposite direction. The other driver got so mad, he threw Garfield into the canal. Just goes to show that anyone can make mistakes on the canal, even someone smart enough to be the president of the United States. That story made me feel like I could be someone important like President Garfield, who used to be a mule skinner, just like me.

The pileup on the canal was more'n we thought. We had to wait our turn lockin' through at Kettle Wells Lock and Red Lock cause there were boats comin' along the canal from the opposite direction, too.

By the time we was comin' up on Boston Village, it was dark and I was lookin' forward to puttin' up the mules for the night. Black shadows covered the towpath. The wind high in the trees made the leaves move, casting odd movement on the towpath. Tonight there was just a sliver of a moon. In some places, it was so dark that only the gleam from the canal water marked the edge of the towpath, and many a mule and driver ran the risk of walking right into that old silver ribbon and drownin' on a night like this one.

There's a cemetery on the river side of the towpath just as you come into the village of Boston, and I never could pass that cemetery without goose flesh crawling all up and down my arms. One time I told Pa that I didn't like drivin' our mules past that cemetery cause they got all nervous and skittish. Pa just laughed at me.

"Why Skinny, if the Lord has a canal in heaven, he'll sure get more than one crew from the souls buried up there in that yard," said Pa. "Canal folks have been buried in that yard for as long as I been runnin' boats. No need to be afraid of the spirits of canal folk, now is there, Skinny? They're just looking out for their own, is all."

After that, I felt a little better about passing that cemetery in the daytime, but I sure didn't like goin' past the place at night. As we approached the place I looked away, afraid that I might see a ghost rise from his dismal grave. So I watched the canal instead, but the mists risin' from the water began to resemble spirits, and I was some glad to finally lock through in Boston, where I was sure we'd tie up for the night.

At Wallace Lock, I was preparin' to unhitch Lookout and Son of a Gun, when I heard Captain Warren callin' to me. Warren jumped off the boat neatly as George snubbed the boat to a stop.

"Don't unhitch the mules yet, Skinny. We had a crew meeting and decided to keep running tonight until we reach Peninsula. There's less traffic on the canal at night, so we can make up some of the time we lost," said Warren.

"Don't expect me to drive these mules at night. It's too dark, not even a moon out to light the towpath. Besides, Ma doesn't like us kids on the towpath at night," I sputtered.

There were all kinds of dangers running a canal boat after dark. Besides the risk of falling into the canal, there was wild animals that came out of the woods to stalk the mules. And sometimes drunks and thieves wandered along the towpath at night, waitin' to jump the canalers and take what they could find.

And then there was Lonesome Lock. If we kept running, we'd have to lock through Lonesome Lock in the middle of the night. Even the heartiest canaler had a healthy fear of Lonesome Lock at night. I sure did. I had to make Warren see sense.

"I'm not drivin Son of a Gun at night--he's too skittish, and he..." I started, hearing the whine in my own voice.

"Scaredy Skinny, why don't you just grow up," Warren shot back at me. "As captain, I order you to drive. Now hitch up those mules. We're gettin' to Peninsula before we tie up, even if it takes us all night." And Warren spun around and headed back to the boat. Then he stopped abruptly and called back to me.

"Hey Skinny! Maybe you'll get lucky and see the naked ghost at Lonesome Lock!" I could hear Warren laughing and laughing as he disappeared into the darkness.

"Take the world, but give me the old canal."

From *The Old Canal*, by Captain Pearl "Skinny" Nye.

Chapter 11

After the canal leaves Boston, the towpath winds its way past a deep swamp known as Stumpy Basin. In the winter, workers harvest ice in the basin, cutting huge blocks of black ice. Then they pack the blocks in sawdust and store it in two ice houses at the southern end of Stumpy Basin. Later in the spring, the ice blocks are taken by canal boat to Cleveland, where it is sold for refrigeration.

I wasn't thinkin' about the ice harvest as we passed through Stumpy Basin on that night, though. It was a warm night, and the tree frogs, crickets and cicadas were loud as we sped along the towpath. I thought I saw something white rise from the swamp, and the goose flesh rose on my arms. Swamp mists could play tricks on your mind. We was comin' up on Lonesome Lock, just on the other side of the Stumpy Basin ice houses.

The swamp smells were stronger at night, and the odor of rotting plants filled my nostrils. Overhead, the tree tops formed a canopy over the towpath, making it so dark I could barely see the mules just a few feet ahead of me. I could hear them though, hear their old broom tails swishing back and forth, and the sounds of their feet on the soft towpath. It made me feel better to know they were with me, cause I'd left Guess aboard the Tom Warren to sleep with Cora.

As we came up beside the icehouse, Son of a Gun, who was the lead mule, came to abrupt stop. Lookout stopped. I stopped. The shadows fidgeted in the evening breeze.

And then out of the darkness, I saw *IT* coming at me on the towpath, all white and floating about a foot above the ground. There was nothing misty about what I saw. It was real and it was on the towpath with me and the mules. Son of a Gun began to fuss. I was shaking so much I had to grip the tow rope for support. My knees began to turn all soft, like I could hardly stand up.

I watched the thing move ahead of me on the towpath, making a side to side motion as it disappeared into the gloom. It disappeared and then came out of the woods in front of me even closer to where me and them old mules still stood. I couldn't move.

The panic came on me like a rolling wave, and then it broke over me and carried me down, down, just like the day I fell into the river and almost drowned. I felt utter terror and the awfulness of everything in my life washed over me--the spells that kept me from going to school, that kept me from being loved by my family. Standing there on that towpath, I felt the years and years of fear still to come, and I was its victim.

And then somewhere inside my head, I heard Cora's voice so close she might have been standing there on the towpath with me, but she wasn't. "Shine a light on the demon of darkness and it will disappear," said Cora's voice, and then suddenly I was able to move.

I let go of the tow rope and approached the spirit. As I got closer, I smelled horseflesh, and briefly I thought it was real funny that a ghost would have any smell at all. My heart was hammerin' in my chest as I neared the thing. I reached out towards it, and touched it and it felt curiously warm and dry in my sweating palm. And then it moved again, so I grabbed it and pulled away the whiteness and it fell away, and I saw that I was not confronting a ghost at all. In my hand I held a sheet just like the one I slept on every night in my bunk on the Tom Warren. I was starin' at the swishin' tail of an old nag. Off in the woods I heard the snickerin' of the town jakes who'd tried to scare me. That old horse just stood there in the middle of the towpath, lookin' kind of confused, not knowing whether he should follow the town jakes or the towpath. I tied him up to a tree on the side of the path, so's Son of a Gun and Lookout would be able to pass him. Them stubborn mules still stood where I'd left them.

We locked through Lonesome Lock without seeing any ghosts. Finally, we tied up in Peninsula, and the next day we made it to Akron where we unloaded the lumber. That night we all went to see Miss Uno's show--it was all Cora talked about for weeks after.

While we were in Akron, I bought myself a notebook, and every night I wrote down everything that happened to us and the Tom Warren. Sometimes, I'd sit in my bunk for two, three hours after supper, just a writin' in that notebook.

One night Ma came in. "Where do you go inside your head when you hole up in here with your pen and paper, Skinny?" she asked me.

"I go home, Ma," I answered.

After she left, I turned to a fresh page and I began to write: *I guess life on a canal boat was just about the best life a boy or girl could ever want...*

The summer that I was twelve was when I finally shook hands with myself and the writing helped me to find out who Skinny Nye was. Three years later, Pa died, and we buried him in Peninsula. Ma and us kids took over runnin' the Tom Warren, though it was gettin' harder and harder to compete with the railroad. People all up and down the canal started to call me "Captain Nye," so one of my life's dreams was fulfilled. My other dream was to live out my life on the canal. Maybe the canal didn't belong to me, but I belonged to the canal. Nothing and no one could ever change that.

Epilogue

Skinny continued to operate the Tom Warren with his mother after his father's death until a flood destroyed the canal in 1913. Though the canal life as Skinny knew it could never return, Captain Nye kept the canal alive through his music and poetry. In his lifetime, he wrote the lyrics to more than 700 songs, most of them singing the praises of the canal. Captain Nye was invited to sing his songs at the National Folk Festival in Washington D.C. in the 1930's and 1940's.

When he was 67, Captain Nye (who was no longer "Skinny" figuratively or literally) decided to return to the canal for good. In 1939, he built a cabin on top of an old Ohio & Erie Canal lock in Roscoe, Ohio. Later, he built an addition to his home, using the rotted out hulk of an abandoned canal boat. He called his home "Camp Charming," and some folks think he did it as a joke on his neighbors who didn't think his home was charming at all. Captain Pearl "Skinny" Nye died in 1950.

The portion of the Ohio & Erie Canal you traveled with Skinny in this book now belongs to the Cuyahoga Valley National Recreation Area. The towpath has been wonderfully restored as a bike/hike path, and markers at the locks tell about the history of the canal. At the Canal Visitor Center in Valley View, you can see a working model of a lock, as well as pictures and exhibits of the days when the Ohio & Erie Canal was the silver ribbon of economic prosperity for the people who worked on it and for those who dwelled along its towpath.

On July 3, 1827, a gala party of dignitaries boarded a canal boat in Akron and arrived in Cleveland the next day to celebrate the opening of the first segment of the Ohio & Erie. The canal era eventually transformed Ohio from a frontier state into one of the world's great industrial centers. (From a color slide by Jane Ann Turzillo.)

This photo shows the Nye family boats which operated in tandem in order to accommodate the large family. Pa Nye is standing on the rear boat, probably holding the hand of son Warren. Ma Nye is seated with one of the younger children. This photo was apparently taken before the family converted the Tom Warren into a freighter and moved to the northern part of the Ohio & Erie Canal to haul lumber south and coal and stone north. (Used with permission of the Canal Society of Ohio, University of Akron Archives).

This photo shows a typical three-cabin freighter with cargo holds in between. Most boats were eighty feet long, fourteen feet wide, and rode low in the water when loaded with cargo. (Used with permission of the Canal Society of Ohio, University of Akron Archives.)

Picnic excursions were common on the Ohio & Erie Canal. This photo shows day trippers aboard the *Akron* on the Ohio & Erie near Cleveland. (Used with permission of the Canal Society of Ohio, University of Akron Archives.)

Because the Ohio & Erie Canal towpath was very narrow, the mule team was hitched in tandem, one behind the other rather than side by side. Here the team is driven by a muleskinner. (From the book **A Photo Album of Ohio's Canal Era, 1825-1913** by Jack Gieck, Kent State University Press, 1988. Used with permission.)

Canal children, including the Nye youngsters, only went to school in winter when the canal was iced over and the boats frozen in. When they weren't attending school, the children enjoyed ice skating on the Ohio & Erie. (Used with permission of the Canal Society of Ohio, University of Akron Archives.)

The remains of Lonesome Lock (Lock #31) can be seen today just north of Peninsula. The men and women who navigated the canal believed this lock to be haunted. (Photo by the author.)

Johnny Cake Lock as it looks today. The lock was named because passengers ate only fried johnny cake (corn bread) for several days while their boat was stuck in the mud. The lock is just north of Akron. (From a color slide by Jane Ann Turzillo.)

Today, portions of the Ohio & Erie Canal towpath have been transformed into a beautiful bike and hike trail that winds through woods, swamps, and farm fields. The towpath between Cleveland and Akron is maintained by the Cuyahoga Valley National Recreation Area. (From a color slide by Jane Ann Turzillo.)

Glossary of Terms and Expressions Used in This Book

Aqueduct
A bridge-like structure that carried the canal and towpath above ground level across a stream or valley.

Balance beam
A long board attached to the lock gate and used to open and close the gate manually.

Bow
Front part of the canal boat.

Bowman
Crew member who helps the canal boat through the lock by snubbing the boat at the bow to keep it from crashing into the lock gates.

Broomtail
Slang term for mule.

Canalers (also canawlers)
Term applied to people who lived and worked on the canal.
This term probably came into general usage after the canal era ended; working canal people of both genders referred to themselves as "boatmen."

Cabin
Enclosed part of the canal boat which housed the cooking and sleeping quarters, as well as the stable.

Captain
Person in charge of the canal boat operations; usually the boat's owner.

Catwalk
A plank or narrow walkway connecting the tops of the cabins. The catwalk spanned the length of the canal boat, allowing the crew to traverse the boat, over the cargo, from one end to the other. Cargo was carried in between the cabins.

Cholera
An infectious disease that causes diarrhea and vomiting, and sometimes, death. The cholera bacteria is usually spread through a bad water supply. Many canal workers died of cholera during an epidemic in 1832, and according to legend, were placed in unmarked graves alongside the canal bed.

Cicadas
Large insects which make shrill buzzing sounds. A mass of cicadas on a hot summer night can make an unforgettable sound that carries in waves across the forest.

Cleveland
The northernmost point of the Ohio & Erie Canal.

Couping stone (also coping stone)
The top stone of a lock.

Cuyahoga River
The Ohio river which runs parallel to the northerly portion of the Ohio & Erie Canal. The Cuyahoga River flows generally from south to north, emptying into Lake Erie at Cleveland.

Deck
The walking area of the canal boat, usually the roofs of the cabins.

Excursion boat (packet)
A canal boat used to carry mainly passengers. Some of these boats were used especially by sightseers and day trippers.

Fitting the lock
Getting the lock ready so that the canal boat could pass through it.

Freighter
A canal boat that carried freight or cargo, such as the Nye's Tom Warren.

Garfield, James
The 20th President of the United States (born 1831, died 1881). As a teenager, Garfield worked as a driver on his uncle's canal boat one summer. He gave up life as a canaler after contracting malaria. Garfield became president and was assassinated in office in 1881.

Gates
Wooden doors which were opened and closed by means of the balance beams. The gates controlled the flow of water into and out of the lock.

Gate paddle
A valve built into a lock gate, which helped control the water flow into or out of the lock. A gate paddle looks like a mini gate built into the larger gate.

Hairpin
The canal boat cook.

Hatch
The door that was cut into the deck, or the top of the cabin. One descended into the cabin on a ladder attached to the cabin wall.

Heel path
The canal bank opposite the tow path.

Jakes (also town jakes)
Term used by canal workers to describe those who lived and worked on land. The canal people felt superior to the townspeople, and vice versa.

Lock
The engineered structure that lowered or raised canal boats between water levels. Components included the lock chamber, lock gates, paddles, and balance beams. Remains of the Ohio & Erie Canal lock walls are clearly visible today, and one working lock operates at the Canal Visitor Center in Valley View, Ohio.

Lock tender
Persons stationed at a lock who assisted the boatmen with locking through. At most, if not all, of the Ohio & Erie Canal locks during the later days of operation, however, boatmen locked through on their own.

Mallard
A common species of wild duck, still seen on the watered parts of the Ohio & and Erie Canal today.

Medicine spoon
A box filled with sawdust or manure. When passed under the leak of a canal boat, the inflow of water pulled the sawdust or manure into the leak, plugging it as the material swelled.

Mouth organ
Another name for a harmonica, ar small musical instrument that makes tones as the player inhales and exhales through its air slots.

Muleskinner
Another term for driver, one who guided the mules or horses along the towpath as the animals pulled the canal boats.

Pilot
A person who was hired to help steer the canal boat through difficult passages. In Akron, for example, pilots would often hire out to help guide boats through the 15-lock staircase through that town.

Portsmouth
The southernmost point of the Ohio & Erie Canal.

Sidecuts
A feeder or branch canal that connected the main canal with a navigable river.

Snubbing post
A stout post around which a crew member wrapped his ropes in order to slow the canal boat as it approached a lock.

Steersman
Person on the canal boat who tended the tiller which steered the craft. The steersman's job was to keep his boat in the middle of the canal channel and to keep the boat from hitting the sides of the lock and aqueduct abutments.

Tiller
A wooden paddle or blade with which the steersman controlled the canal boat.

Towpath
The walking path from which the muleskinner or driver and his animals pulled the boat. The animals were attached to the canal boat with a set of ropes called the tow line. The driver usually walked along behind the animals.

Weigh lock
A special lock with a set of scales to measure the weight of the canal boat. Fees were assessed according to the weight of the cargo.

Wiffletree
A harness-type outfit with which the towing animals were hitched to the towline.

Selected Bibliography: Ohio & Erie Canal

Books

The Canaller's Song Book by William Hullfish (American Canal and Transportation Center, 1987).

The Ohio Canals by Frank Wilcox, edited by William McGill (Kent State University Press, 1969).

The Ohio & Erie Canal, A Glossary of Terms by Terry K. Woods (Kent State University Press, 1995).

A Photo Album of Ohio's Canal Era, 1825-1913 by Jack Gieck (Kent State University Press, 1988).

Articles

"The Canal Corridor," Akron Beacon Journal, April 15, 1994, p. A14.

"Captain Pearl Nye's Ohio Canal Songs" by Richard Swain. The Gamut, Cleveland State University, Fall 1983.

"To Make Canals Live Again in Print is His Ambition; Pearl R. Nye, Poet, Once Was Captain on 'Ditch' Himself" by John Botzum. The Akron Times Press, March 8, 1936.

"Old Canal Even Had Its Snake Charmer, Captain Nye, Veteran Boatman, Recalls" by Helen Waterhouse, May 28, 1936.

"Winter at Stumpy Basin" by Fred Bishop. Towpaths, The Canal Society of Ohio, vol. XVI, no. 1, p. 6.

Unpublished Manuscripts

"The Life and Times of Pearl R. Nye, Ballader, Historian, Survivor" by Terry K. Woods. Unpublished manuscript, Summit County Historical Society/University of Akron Archival Department, n.d.

"Take a Trip on the Canal If You Want to Have Fun" by Pearl R. Nye. Unpublished, handwritten manuscript, Summit County Historical Society/University of Akron Archival Department, 1939.

Maps

Ohio & Erie Canal Corridor Guide, produced by the Education Committee, Ohio & Erie Canal Corridor Coalition, Canal Fulton, Ohio, n.d.

The Ohio & Erie Canal Towpath Trail, map and text produced by The Cuyahoga Valley Trails Council for the National Park Service, n.d.

Guide to Ohio Historic Canals, Preserved and Restored Sites with Map of Ohio Canal System, 1825-1913, Canal Society of Ohio, n.d.